This Little Tiger book belongs to:

6'
_____

_____

_____

For all children
(and parents) who
could do with a
good night's sleep
- S M

Love to Jonty and Ros -
thanks for your never-ending support
- N E

LITTLE TIGER PRESS

1 The Coda Centre, 189 Munster Road, London SW6 6AW

www.littletiger.co.uk

First published in Great Britain 2013

This edition published 2014

Text copyright © Sue Mongredien 2013

Illustrations copyright © Nick East 2013

Sue Mongredien and Nick East have asserted their rights to be identified

as the author and illustrator of this work under the Copyright,

Designs and Patents Act, 1988

A CIP catalogue record for this book is available from the British Library

ISBN 978-1-84895-299-7

Printed in China

LTP/1400/0759/1113

2 4 6 8 10 9 7 5 3 1

Little Tiger
Press

Sue
Mongredien

Nick East

Harry
AND THE
MONSTER

On Monday night, Harry had a bad dream —
a bad, scary dream about a bad,
scary monster.

"ROOOAARR!"

went the monster.

"Aargh!"
shouted Harry, waking everyone up.

On Tuesday night, Harry didn't want to go to bed.

"What if the monster comes back?" he said.

"Hmmm," said Mum. "Try imagining him
with a pair of **pink pants** on his head.
You'll laugh so much it won't be scary."

Harry went to sleep.
He dreamed about his birthday.
It was a **good** dream.
But then . . .

the monster

burst in.

Harry quickly dreamed up the
pinkest pants possible . . .
right on the monster's head!

The monster was angry.

"WHO PA

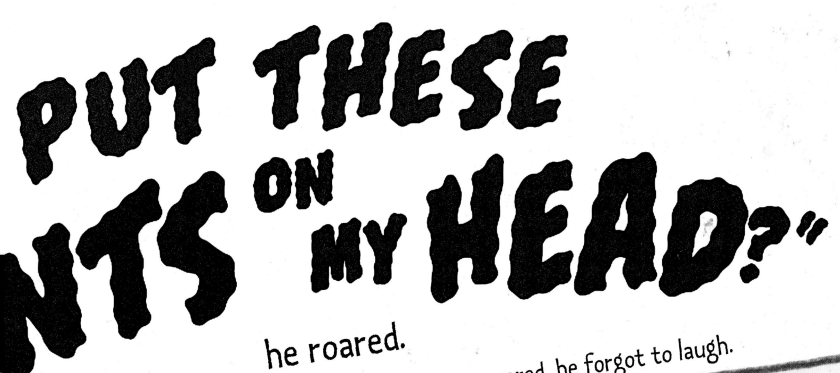

PUT THESE
NTS ON MY HEAD?"

he roared.

Harry was so scared, he forgot to laugh.

"Aaargh!"

shouted Harry, waking everyone up.

On **Wednesday** night, Harry made Dad check under the bed.

"Harry," said Dad, "if you dream about that monster again, just imagine him stuck in some jelly. Then you'll be able to run away."

Harry went to sleep. He dreamed about playing in the park. It was a **good** dream.

But then the **monster** popped up.

Harry quickly dreamed that the monster
was stuck in **wibbly-wobbly jelly**.
The monster was **furious!**

"WHO MADE THIS JELLY?" he roared.

Harry was so scared, he forgot to run away.

"Aaaargh!" shouted Harry, waking everyone up.

On **Thursday** night, Harry said he wasn't at all tired, not even **one tiny bit.**

"I've got an idea," said Mum. "Just imagine tickling that monster with a **big fluffy feather.** He'll giggle so much, he won't be able to roar!"

Harry went to sleep.
He dreamed about Christmas.
It was a **good** dream.

But
then
the
monster
clattered
in.

Harry quickly dreamed up a fluffy feather.
Then he began tickling the monster.
The monster giggled so much, he
toppled into the Christmas tree.

Prickles jabbed his bottom.

On Friday night, Harry was nowhere
to be seen.
"The scary monster's going to get me,"
came a voice from under the covers.
Dad patted the Harry-shaped lump.

"Do you know what monsters are scared of?"
said Dad. "Cross mummies. So just imagine
your mum telling him off. Then he'll be the
scared one!"

Harry went to sleep.

But
then

He dreamed about playing trains. It was a **good** dream.

the
monster
rode in.

Harry quickly dreamed up a **cross mum.**

"Look at the STATE

Cross Mum yelled at the monster.

"What a MESS you've all over the car Clean yourself this minute!"

Suddenly the monster didn't look so scary any more.

Harry felt sorry for the monster so he made
Cross Mum disappear.

"**PHEW,**" gulped the monster.
"SHE WAS **REALLY** SCARY!"

Then the monster looked around.

"*I'M SORRY I SPOILED YOUR TRAIN SET,*" he said, in a
quiet little voice.

"That's OK," said Harry. "I can dream up a better one."

So Harry and the monster played happily
for the rest of the night.

And on Saturday morning...

. . . everyone had a lie-in.